GH00730043

THE WORLDLY TEACHER

A STORY OF MISSION, REFLECTION, AND COMMUNITY

BY: ERIC D. NELSON

Illustrated by: FLEANCE FORKUO

Legacy of

FRANCES (FANNY) MARION JACKSON COPPIN

Published by Melanin Origins

PO Box 122123; Arlington, TX 76012

Copyright 2022

First Edition

The author asserts the moral right under the Copyright, Designs and Patents Act of 1988 to be identified as the author of this work.

This novel is a work of fiction. The names, characters and incidents portrayed in the work, other than those clearly in the public domain, are of the author's imagination and are not to be construed as real. Any resemblance to actual persons, living or dead, events or localities, is entirely coincidental.

Library of Congress Control Number: 2022910720

ISBN: 979-8-9864006-0-0 hardback

ISBN: 979-8-9864006-1-7 paperback

ISBN: 979-8-9864006-4-8 ebook

I plant this book as a seed in the world. This book is for the Black leaders that are rarely and vaguely discussed in schools. To tell a story, you must have characters. So, who are the characters of our history? Frances (Fanny) Marion Jackson Coppin is one of our pioneering characters in our story of education. Readers do not stop with reading this book. Continue to learn. Grow like a plant and let knowledge water you.

ERIC D. NELSON

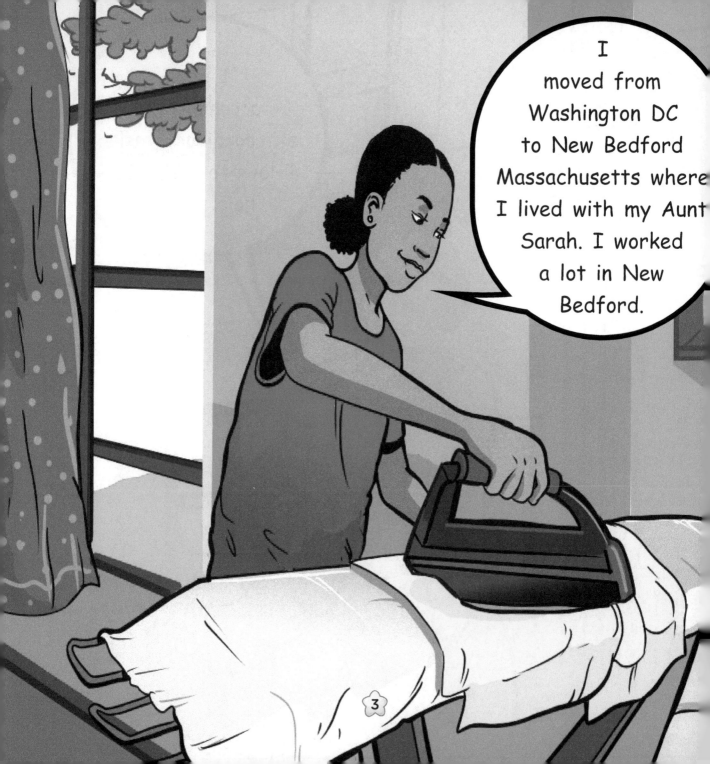

I was introduced to the subject of teaching at the Rhode Island State Normal School and learned to speak French. *"I said to myself, is it possible that teaching can be made so interesting as this! But, having finished the course of study there, I felt that I had just begun to learn"*.

In 1837, the Friends of Philadelphia established the Institute for Colored Youth, today known as Cheyney University. I was head of the girl's department.

Working with the Institute for Colored Youth (ICY), I created and taught classes in reviewing English studies, theory of teaching, school management and methods.

In less than five years after graduating from Oberlin College, I was head of the girl's department, spearheaded the establishment of an industrial department, worked with The Christian Recorder (edited and published by colored men), and became the principal of the Institute for Colored Youth.

"After having spent thirty-seven years in the school room, laboring to give a correct start in life to the youth that came under my influence, it was indeed, to me, a fortunate incident to finish my active work right in Africa, the home of the ancestors of those whose lives I had endeavored to direct."

It was a privilege to travel the world speaking with and teaching all. To go to Africa, it was pleasant to contribute to the life on the land of my ancestors.

20

ABOUT THE AUTHOR

ERIC D. NELSON is a service-leader. He believes serving others is a gift all can do with life. He serves through teaching, modeling, writing, and cooking. The Worldly Teacher is Nelson's first children's picture book vividly narrates the life of **Frances (Fanny) Marion Jackson Coppin**.

He is an alumnus of Coppin State University, Baltimore, Maryland, where he earned a degree in Elementary Education. He is a contributing poet to Kevin Powell's Writing Workshop's 2020: ***The Year That Changed America.*** He seeks that readers connect with his books and move with purpose.

Lightning Source UK Ltd.
Milton Keynes UK
UKHW050606290722
406558UK00002B/45

9 798986 400600